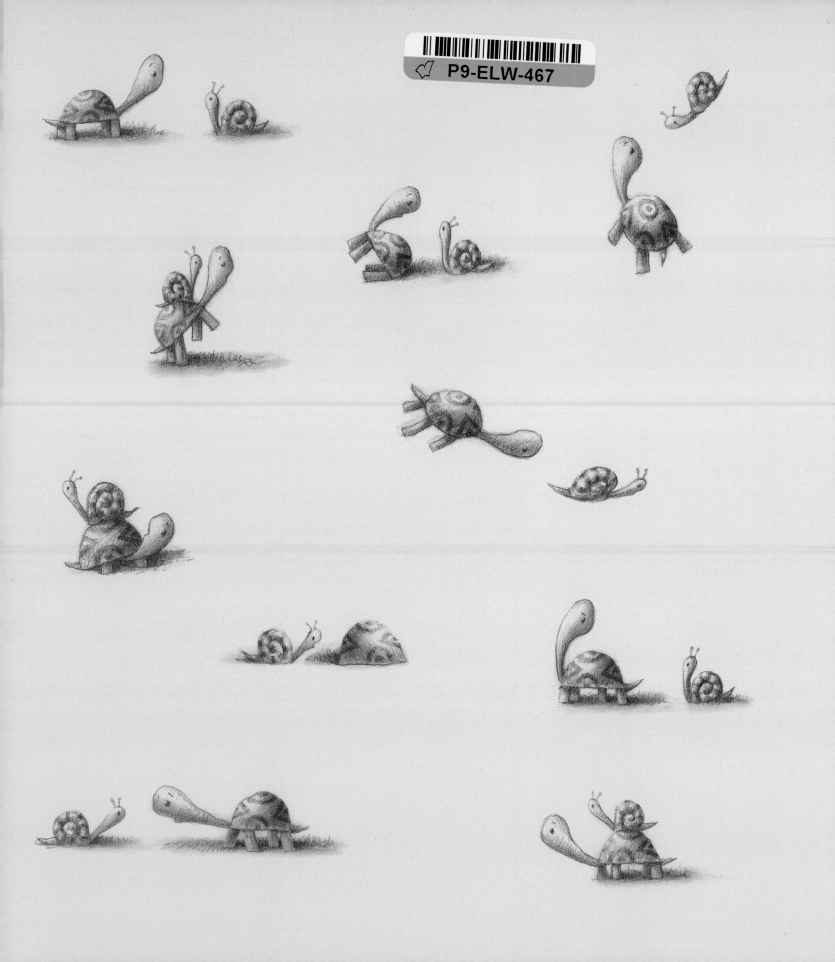

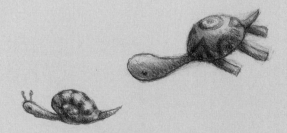

"Once upon a time there was a lake.
And there was a log on the bottom of it."
—Unknown Legend

For Virgil,
who sang this to Tracy over and over
and over as she was growing up!

Philomel Books
an imprint of Penguin Random House LLC
Visit us at penguinrandomhouse.com

Copyright © 2018 by Loren Long.

Library of Congress Cataloging-in-Publication Data
Names: Long, Loren, author, illustrator. | Title: There's a hole in the log on the bottom of the lake / Loren
Long. | Other titles: There is a hole in the log on the bottom of the lake | Description: New York, NY: Philomel
Books, [2018] | Summary: An adaptation of the traditional folk song "There's a Hole in the Bottom of the Sea,"
with additional repetition and tongue twisters. Includes sheet music. | Identifiers: LCCN 2018019088 | ISBN
9780399163999 (hardback) | ISBN 9780698174573 (ebook) | Subjects: LCSH: Children's songs—United States—
Texts. | CYAC: Songs. | Humorous songs. | BISAC: JUVENILE FICTION / Humorous Stories. | JUVENILE FICTION /
Performing Arts / Music. | JUVENILE FICTION / Animals / Frogs & Toads. | Classification: LCC PZ8.3.L8513
The 2018 | DDC 782.42083—dc23 | LC record available at https://lccn.loc.gov/2018019088

Manufactured in China by RR Donnelley Asia Printing Solutions Ltd.
ISBN 9780399163999
Special Markets ISBN 9781984837264 Not for Resale
3 5 7 9 10 8 6 4 2

Edited by Michael Green. Design by Ellice M. Lee.
Music arranged by Cheryl Eissing. Text set in Aram ITC Std.
The art was done in acrylic and colored pencils.

This Imagination Library edition is published by Penguin Young Readers, a division
of Penguin Random House, exclusively for Dolly Parton's Imagination Library,
a not-for-profit program designed to inspire a love of reading and learning, sponsored
in part by The Dollywood Foundation. Penguin's trade editions of this work are
available wherever books are sold.

THERE'S A HOLE IN THE LOG

IN THE

LOG

ON THE BOTTOM OF THE LAKE

LOREN LONG

PHILOMEL BOOKS

THERE'S A **LOG** ON THE BOTTOM OF THE LAKE.

THERE'S A **LOG** ON THE BOTTOM OF THE LAKE.

THERE'S A LOG?
THERE'S A LOG!

"It's just
a piece of
rotten wood."

THERE'S A **LOG LOG LOG**
THERE'S A **LOG** ON THE BOTTOM OF THE LAKE.

THERE'S A **HOLE** IN THE **LOG** ON THE BOTTOM OF THE LAKE.

THERE'S A **HOLE** IN THE **LOG** ON THE BOTTOM OF THE LAKE.

"A whole what? It just looks empty to me."

THERE'S A HOLE?
THERE'S A HOLE!

THERE'S A HOLE HOLE HOLE IN THE LOG LOG LOG

THERE'S A HOLE IN THE LOG ON THE BOTTOM OF THE LAKE.

"Dial 911! Turtle on its back! Emergency! Turtle freaking out!"

THERE'S A FROG IN THE HOLE
IN THE LOG ON THE BOTTOM OF THE LAKE.

THERE'S A **FROG** IN THE **HOLE** IN THE **LOG** ON THE BOTTOM OF THE LAKE.

"Hey, look!
It's the guys.
Wait for us!"

THERE'S A FROG?
THERE'S A FROG!

THERE'S A FROG FROG FROG
IN THE HOLE HOLE HOLE
IN THE LOG LOG LOG

THERE'S A FROG IN THE HOLE IN THE LOG
ON THE BOTTOM OF THE LAKE.

"Please just try
to fit in this
time. NO MORE
SNAIL TALK!"

THERE'S A HAIR ON THE FROG IN THE HOLE IN THE LOG ON THE BOTTOM OF THE LAKE.

THERE'S A **HAIR** ON THE **FROG** IN THE **HOLE** IN THE **LOG** ON THE BOTTOM OF THE LAKE.

"Okay, I get it.
Now you're too cool
for school. Well,
don't forget Mr.
Turtle back here!"

THERE'S A HAIR?
THERE'S A HAIR!

"Ew. Is there really a
hair on that frog?"

THERE'S A HAIR HAIR HAIR
ON THE FROG FROG FROG
IN THE HOLE HOLE HOLE
IN THE LOG LOG LOG

THERE'S A HAIR ON THE FROG IN THE HOLE IN THE LOG ON THE BOTTOM OF THE LAKE.

"It gets worse. His hair has bugs."

THERE'S A **FLY** ON THE **HAIR** ON THE **FROG** IN THE **HOLE** IN THE **LOG** ON THE BOTTOM OF THE LAKE.

THERE'S A FLY?
THERE'S A FLY!

"Oh, great! I'll never get this song out of my head."

THERE'S A FLY FLY FLY
ON THE HAIR HAIR HAIR
ON THE FROG FROG FROG
IN THE HOLE HOLE HOLE
IN THE LOG LOG LOG

THERE'S A FLY ON THE HAIR ON THE FROG
IN THE HOLE IN THE LOG ON THE BOTTOM OF THE LAKE.

THERE'S A GNAT ON THE FLY ON THE HAIR ON THE FROG IN THE HOLE IN THE LOG ON THE BOTTOM OF THE LAKE.

"Ugh, now his bug has bugs?"

THERE'S A GNAT ON THE FLY ON THE HAIR ON THE FROG IN THE HOLE IN THE LOG ON THE BOTTOM OF THE LAKE.

THERE'S A GNAT?
THERE'S A GNAT!

THERE'S A GNAT GNAT GNAT
ON THE FLY FLY FLY
ON THE HAIR HAIR HAIR
ON THE FROG FROG FROG
IN THE HOLE HOLE HOLE
IN THE LOG LOG LOG

THERE'S A GNAT ON THE FLY ON THE
HAIR ON THE FROG IN THE
HOLE IN THE LOG
ON THE BOTTOM OF THE LAKE.

"This place is weird.
I'm out of here!"

THERE'S A **FISH** NEAR THE **GNAT** ON THE **FLY**
ON THE **HAIR** ON THE **FROG** IN THE **HOLE**
IN THE **LOG** ON THE BOTTOM OF THE LAKE.

THERE'S A FISH NEAR THE GNAT ON THE FLY ON THE HAIR ON THE FROG IN THE HOLE IN THE LOG ON THE BOTTOM OF THE LAKE.

"Uh-oh..."

THERE'S A . . .

UH-OH.

CHOMP, SNAP, GULP!

THERE'S A FISH ON THE BOTTOM OF THE LAKE.
THERE'S A FISH ON THE BOTTOM OF THE LAKE.
THERE'S A FISH?
JUST A FISH.
THERE'S A FISH ON THE BOTTOM OF THE LAKE . . .

There's a Hole in the Log on the Bottom of the Lake

VERSE 1

There's a log on the bottom of the lake.
There's a log on the bottom of the lake.
There's a LOG? There's a LOG!
There's a log log log
There's a log on the bottom of the lake.

VERSE 2

There's a hole in the log on the bottom of the lake.
There's a hole in the log on the bottom of the lake.
There's a HOLE? There's a HOLE!
There's a hole hole hole
   in the log log log
There's a hole in the log on the bottom of the lake.

VERSE 3

There's a frog in the hole in the log on the bottom of the lake.
There's a frog in the hole in the log on the bottom of the lake.
There's a FROG? There's a FROG!
There's a frog frog frog
   in the hole hole hole
   in the log log log
There's a frog in the hole in the log on the bottom of the lake.

VERSE 4

There's a hair on the frog in the hole in the log on the bottom
   of the lake.
There's a hair on the frog in the hole in the log on the bottom
   of the lake.
There's a HAIR? There's a HAIR!
There's a hair hair hair
   on the frog frog frog
   in the hole hole hole
   in the log log log
There's a hair on the frog in the hole in the log on the bottom
   of the lake.

VERSE 5

There's a fly on the hair on the frog in the hole in the log on
   the bottom of the lake.
There's a fly on the hair on the frog in the hole in the log on
   the bottom of the lake.
There's a FLY? There's a FLY!
There's a fly fly fly
   on the hair hair hair
   on the frog frog frog
   in the hole hole hole
   in the log log log
There's a fly on the hair on the frog in the hole in the log on
   the bottom of the lake.

VERSE 6

There's a gnat on the fly on the hair on the frog in the hole in
   the log on the bottom of the lake.
There's a gnat on the fly on the hair on the frog in the hole in
   the log on the bottom of the lake.
There's a GNAT? There's a GNAT!
There's a gnat gnat gnat
   on the fly fly fly
   on the hair hair hair
   on the frog frog frog
   in the hole hole hole
   in the log log log
There's a gnat on the fly on the hair on the frog in the hole in
   the log on the bottom of the lake.

VERSE 7

There's a fish near the gnat on the fly on the hair on the frog in
   the hole in the log on the bottom of the lake.
There's a fish near the gnat on the fly on the hair on the frog in
   the hole in the log on the bottom of the lake.
There's a . . . Uh-oh.
CHOMP, SNAP, GULP!
There's a fish on the bottom of the lake.
There's a fish on the bottom of the lake.
There's a FISH? Just a FISH.
There's a fish on the bottom of the lake . . .

"For some reason, now I have
the urge to take guitar lessons."